Mouse's Marriage

7124

For Helen and Thomas

PUFFIN BOOKS
Published by the Penguin Group
Penguin Books USA Inc.,
375 Hudson Street, New York, New York 10014, U.S.A.
Penguin Books Ltd, 27 Wrights Lane, London W8 5TZ, England
Penguin Books Australia Ltd, Ringwood, Victoria, Australia
Penguin Books Canada Ltd, 10 Alcorn Avenue, Toronto, Ontario, Canada M4V 3B2
Penguin Books (N.Z.) Ltd, 182–190 Wairau Road, Auckland 10, New Zealand

Penguin Books Ltd, Registered Offices: Harmondsworth, Middlesex, England

First published in Australia by Lothian Publishing Company Pty Ltd., 1985
First published in the United States of America by Viking Penguin Inc., 1986
Published in Puffin Books 1988
5 7 9 10 8 6 4
Illustrations copyright © Junko Morimoto, 1985
Adaptation copyright © Anne Bower Ingram, 1985
All rights reserved

LIBRARY OF CONGRESS CATALOGING IN PUBLICATION DATA
Morimoto, Junko.
Mouse's marriage/illustrated by Junko Morimoto.
p. cm.
Summary. A mouse couple, in search of the mightiest husband for
their daughter, approach the sun, the clouds, the wind, and a wall,
before the unexpected victor finally appears.
ISBN 0-14-050678-0 (pbk.)
[1. Folklore—Japan. 2. Mice—Folklore. 3. Marriage—Folklore.] I. Title.
[PZ8.1.M825MO 1988] 398.2'45293233'0—dc19 87-34573 [E]

Printed in the United States of America

MOUSE'S MARRIAGE

Illustrated by Junko Morimoto

PUFFIN BOOKS

Once, long ago, there lived
an elderly mouse couple.
They had
a very beautiful daughter,
who they loved very much
and, because she was
their only child,
they wanted her to have
the best and mightiest husband
in the world.

So they set off to find him.

First they asked the Sun.
"We think you are the best
and mightiest in the world,"
they said to the Sun.
"Will you marry
our beautiful daughter?"

The Sun beamed down on them,
but just then . . .

a big fluffy Cloud
passed over the Sun
covering him up.

"Oh, Cloud,"
said the Mice,
"We think you must be the best
and mightiest in the world.
Will you marry
our beautiful daughter?"

The Cloud nodded wisely,
but just then . . .

the Wind came rushing in
and blew the Cloud
right across the sky.

"Oh, Wind,"
said the Mice,
"We think you must be the best
and mightiest in the world.
Will you marry
our beautiful daughter?"

The Wind blew very hard,
but just then . . .

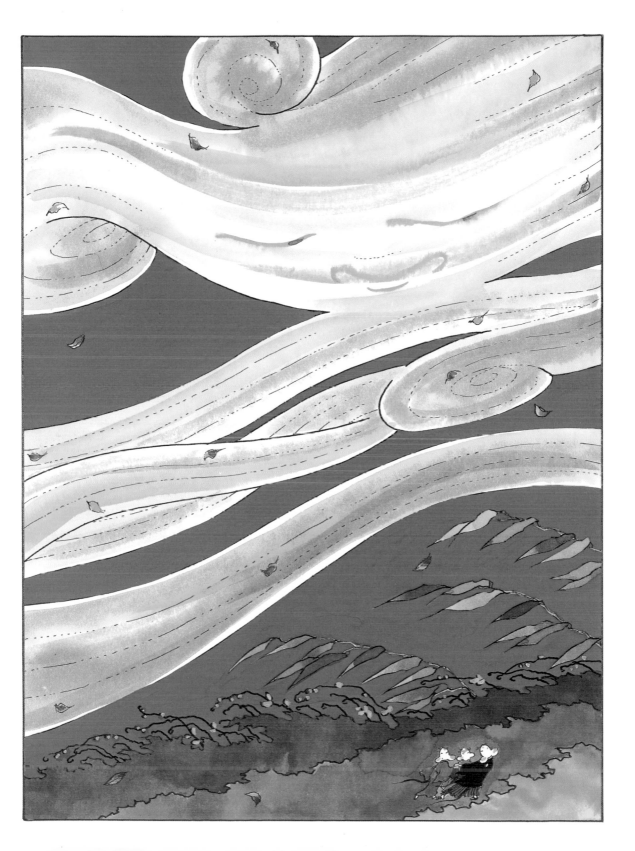

the Wind was stopped by a Wall.

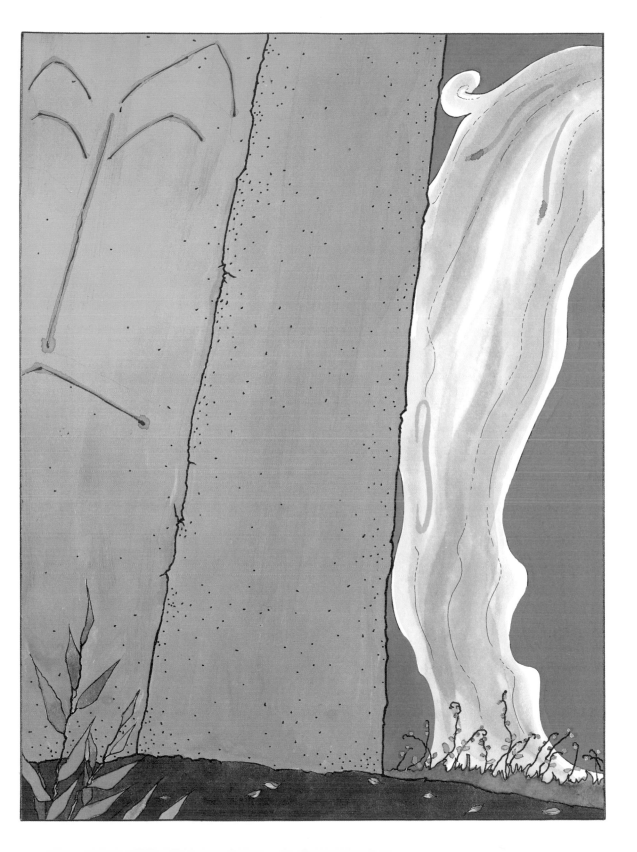

"Oh, Wall,"
said the Mice,
"We think you must be the best
and mightiest in the world.
Will you marry
our beautiful daughter?"

The Wall smiled down
on the Mice,
but just then . . .

the Wall began to crack.
Out tunnelled some Mice.

"Look at that,"
said the parents.
"We Mice are the best
and mightiest of all . . .

Our daughter shall marry a mouse."

And so she did.